JOLLY ROGER
AND THE
UNDERWATER
TREASURE

D1634357

Illustrated by

CHRIS FISHER

Hodder
Children's
Books

a division of Hodder Headline plc

For John Waldren
and all the staff of
Bishop Road Primary School
With love and thanks Viv and Isobel

To Frances, Jack and Richard
Chris Fisher

Text copyright © 1995 Vivian French
Illustrations copyright © 1995 Chris Fisher

First published in Great Britain in 1995
by Hodder Children's Books

The right of Vivian French to be identified as the Author of the Work has been asserted
by her in accordance with the Copyright, Designs and Patents Act 1988.

10   9   8   7   6   5   4   3   2   1

A Catalogue record for this book is available from the British Library

ISBN 0340 61952X

Printed and bound in Great Britain by Cox & Wyman Ltd, Reading, Berks.

Hodder Children's Books
A Division of Hodder Headline plc
338 Euston Road
London NW1 3BH

CHAPTER ONE

"Yo ho ho
and here we go!
Swing all the barrels
up from down below!
An ikky chocky
bicky
can really hit the
spot
So MUNCH 'EM!
CRUNCH 'EM!"
and gobble up the lot!

Jolly Roger peered over the edge of the crow's nest at the pirate crew below.

"They sound very cheerful," he said suspiciously. "What are they up to?"

Captain Jennifer Jellyfish Jones laughed and banged him on the back. "They're just happy," she said. "Why don't you climb down and sing with them?"

First Mate Mutt grinned, and Sea Dog Williams wagged his tail.

"Cluck!" said Polly Chicken.

"Go on," said Mutt. "It'll be good for crew morale."

Roger went very pale. "MUST I?" he asked, and he clutched at the edge of the crow's nest. "I didn't think singing with the crew was part of my job. I'd NEVER EVER EVER have come to sea if you'd told me I had to sing. Besides," he swallowed nervously, "I don't know the tune."

Captain Jenny folded her arms and tried to look stern.

"Well," she said, "maybe I'll let you off this time. But just remember – next time we need a volunteer – "

Jolly Roger nodded wildly. "ANYTHING!!!" he promised, "absolutely ANYTHING! ANYTHING except singing."

Jenny shook his hand. "It's a deal!" And she winked at First Mate Mutt as Roger sank to the floor in relief. Sea Dog Williams washed his face to help him recover, and Polly fanned him with her feathers.

Down below the singing grew louder and louder.

Strawberry!
Peppermint!
Custard cream!
Everyone is a pirate's dream
Munch 'em by the handful,
crunch 'em by the score,
burst all your buttons boys,
and gobble up some more!

Mutt raised an eyebrow and leant over the crow's nest edge. "Actually," he said, "I think Jolly Roger was right. They ARE up to something. They're up to eating ALL the ship's biscuits . . . and it looks as if they've been at it for AGES. Look at those empty barrels!"

"WHAT????" Captain Jennifer Jellyfish Jones straightened her pirate's hat and pulled her eye patch into position. "Stealing ship's stores? On MY ship?" She slid down the rigging and onto the deck, landing with a thump right beside Foxy Ratt. Foxy coughed loudly, and pulled himself upright.

"Morning, Cap'n!" said Foxy through a mouthful of crumbs. "Er . . . was you wanting something, as it were?"

Captain Jennifer Jellyfish Jones was not taken in by Foxy Ratt's slimy smile. She knew her evil, wicked and blackhearted pirates only too well, and she knew that Foxy Ratt was one of the evillest, wickedest and most blackhearted.

"Yes, Foxy, I WAS wanting something," she snapped. "I want all the crew in line NOW. Biscuits are for BIRTHDAYS and TREATS, and that's why I keep them under lock and key. I'll have no biscuit stealing on MY ship, and I want to make sure the crew knows all about it!" And she blew her whistle as loudly as she could.

wheeee!!

"WHEEEEEEEEEE!"

Foxy choked on a crumb, and his beady little eyes flickered over the crew where they sat crouched over the last remaining biscuit barrel.

"SSSSSST! YOU LOT! GET UP!!!!!"

Toothy Thomas burped. A button PINGED off Long Jon Mustard's shirt front and rattled across the deck. None of the other pirates moved an inch. Their beards were full of

Ping!

biscuit crumbs and their stomachs were bulging. Their faces were smeared with chocolate, jam, and vanilla cream, and more than one or two were beginning to take on a greenish tinge.

"I think I feels sick," said Toothy in a feeble voice.

"I SEE," said Jenny, and her voice was cold. "Not a single barrel left untouched! First Mate Mutt, Jolly Roger, Sea Dog Williams, Polly - please be kind enough to join me on deck!"

As Mutt, Roger and Sea Dog Williams scrambled down the ropes and Polly flapped onto the deck, Sniffy Smith licked his sticky fingers and reached for one last biscuit. He was so full he could hardly move, and as he staggered to his feet his huge stomach bumped into the barrel. It slid away, rolled under the rail and splashed overboard.

"Oh No! My crunchy cracker!" Sniffy wailed. "My one last crunchy cracker! Come back! Come back to Sniffy!" And Sniffy Smith rushed across the deck of the Ghastly Ghoul and hurled himself into the sea.

"WHEEEEEEEEEEEEE!"

Captain Jenny blew her whistle again as she, Mutt and Roger ran to the rail. Sea Dog Williams barked wildly.

"Quick, someone!" Jenny shouted. "SNIFFY CAN'T SWIM! We need a volunteer!"

"Me! Me! I volunteer!" And Jolly
Roger swung himself over the rail and
into the sea before anyone else had
time to think.

"Wow!" said Mutt as he watched
Roger bob up to the surface in the
middle of a large wave. "I never knew
Jolly Roger was so brave! But what's he
doing now?"

"I think," Jenny said, and her voice
sounded rather odd, "he's sinking. I'm not
sure that he can swim either." She stood
up straight. "LET GO THE ANCHOR!"

There was a buzz of action. The emergency had stirred up Toothy Thomas and Long Jon Mustard, and with a rattle and a clank the chain ran out and the anchor splashed into the sea.

"There's our Sniffy!" Toothy Thomas was peering into the grey blue water. "OI! SNIFFY! Have you found your last crunchy cracker?"

"HELP! HELP!" Sniffy was waving his arms frantically. "I CAN'T SWIM!"

First Mate Mutt grabbed a coil of rope. "Here!" He flung it out into the waves, and Sniffy seized the end.

"PULL!" yelled Mutt, and he and

Sea Dog Williams began hauling the dripping Sniffy from the waves.

Meanwhile Captain Jenny was staring into the water. "Where's Roger?" she asked, "where's good old Jolly Roger?"

CHAPTER TWO

Jolly Roger was rather wondering that himself. He seemed to have been sinking for a very long time, and he felt that it was probably time to go back up to the surface.

Roger opened his eyes. His feet had touched something; something solid. He peered around him through the water.

Up above his head he could see the hull of the Ghastly Ghoul looming large and dark. All around were weeds and brightly coloured fish peering curiously at him. Beneath him was sand, and something that looked oddly familiar.

"Why!" Roger squinted through the water. "It's a SHIP! It must be a wreck. But what's that shining down there?" He tried to peer into the darkness, but suddenly realised that he needed to breathe.

"AAAGH!" he gurgled. "AAAAGH!" And bubbles burst all around him and fizzed up to the surface.

The bubbles were what Captain
Jennifer Jellyfish Jones had been
waiting for. With a loud shout she
kicked off her seaboots and dived into
the sea.

Swimming strongly she shot
through the water,
down and down and . . .
there was Jolly Roger.

Jenny
grabbed him by
the jacket. Roger did not move. He
seemed to be firmly stuck to the sea
bed. Jenny dived lower, and saw Roger
was wearing her second pair of
seaboots; her huge, solid metal toed
sea boots. She waved her arms in front

18

of Roger's purple face and pointed wildly at his feet. Then she tugged at him again - and as she did so he gave a wriggle and shook the boots off. Together they burst up to the surface, Roger coughing and spluttering as their two heads appeared glistening wet in the sunshine. First Mate Mutt cheered loudly and flung them a rope.

"CLUCK!" shrieked Polly Chicken. "CLUCK!"

"WOOF! WOOF!" barked Sea Dog Williams.

Foxy Ratt scowled behind the mast. "Wot a pity," he muttered.

"PHEW!" Captain Jenny was back on deck towelling herself dry. "How are you feeling, Roger?"

Roger was staring into the distance, a strange look on his face.

"JOLLY ROGER! Are you all right?"

Roger shook himself, and sat up straight. "Didn't you SEE it?" he asked.

"See what?"

"GOLD!!!!! GLITTERY STUFF!!!!! HEAPS AND HEAPS AND HEAPS OF IT! Down there! In that wreck!"

Captain Jennifer Jellyfish Jones, First Mate Mutt, Sea Dog Williams, Polly and the entire pirate crew of the Ghastly Ghoul froze. They stared at Jolly Roger.

"TREASURE!" everyone breathed.

"TREASURE!"

"Treasure for us all!"

"We'll all be RICH!!!!"

"HURRAH!!!!!!!!!!!!!!!!!!!!" Sniffy and Toothy grabbed arms and began dancing in a circle.

"GOLD! RUBIES! DI'MONDS! PEARLS!" yelled Toothy.

"Better than barrels and BARRELS of bikkies!" chortled Sniffy.

"Ha ha!" sniggered Foxy Ratt.

Captain Jennifer Jellyfish Jones stamped her foot and swirled her cutlass.

"JUST ONE MOMENT!" she said fiercely.

Toothy and Sniffy stopped and stared.

"Stealing ship's stores," said Jenny, "is a TERRIBLE crime. There's not ONE of you deserves so much as a SNIFF of the treasure. In fact, I'm thinking of throwing you ALL overboard to feed the sharks."

"Yum! Yum!"

Every pirate on board
suddenly went pale.

"BUT," Jenny went on,
"you are all VERY LUCKY.
For once I'm going to give
you a second chance. It seems we have
treasure in sight. If you all work VERY
HARD maybe - just maybe - I'll change
my mind."

Every pirate but one stood up
straight and tried to look hardworking.
Behind them Foxy Ratt sneered
silently.

"There ain't no sharks in these 'ere
parts," he muttered under his breath.
"Never has been, never will be. Now, I
wonders where my water wings are?"
And Foxy slipped silently away.

Captain Jennifer Jellyfish Jones
turned to First Mate Mutt.
"Any ideas?" she asked.
Mutt was looking

22

thoughtful. "I think," he said, "we need some kind of underwater machine. It's too risky to dive down for the treasure . . . I'm sure this is shark territory. Just let me try out a few ideas . . . can you pass me over two of those empty biscuit barrels? And fetch me a couple of hammocks . . . and a few dozen cannon balls . . . and rope . . . and does anyone have any rubber gloves? Oh, and the hose pipe from the bilges and some milk bottles would be useful . . ."

CHAPTER THREE

The whole crew settled themselves down comfortably to watch Mutt building his machine.

"OI!" said Roger, "what's all this?"

Long Jon Mustard smiled widely. "We likes to watch First Mate Mutt at work, sir."

"'Specially when we don't have to work ourselves," said Sniffy brightly.

"Well, well," said Captain Jennifer Jones. "We can't have that, can we, Sniffy? Now, let me think . . . And Jenny walked slowly round the deck. As she walked she fingered the blade of her cutlass, and the crew watched her doubtfully. "I know! Tell me the answer to a question. Next time someone has a birthday, what shall I give them as a treat?"

There was a long silence, only broken by the sound of Mutt sawing and hammering.

"Exactly," said Jenny. "So I think that you'd better get busy. I want every single one of you on parade in TWO minutes with clean hands, an apron and a wooden spoon . . . and we'll make enough biscuits to fill up ALL those barrels!"

Jenny nodded, and swung her cutlass round her head in a casual sort of way. "Well," she said, "put it like this. We've got time to fill in before we can start collecting the treasure. Either you can make biscuits, or you can go overboard. In bits. I need some cutlass practise."

There was a wild rush below decks.

Ten minutes later quite a clean row
of pirates was standing in front of
several large bowls of flour and milk
and butter and sugar and eggs. They
were taking it in turns to mix and stir
and beat and whisk. Polly was in
charge, and Sea Dog Williams was
helping out. Roger was checking
recipes, and reading the long words
for Toothy Thomas.

"Strike me pink!" said Long Jon Mustard, "and blow me down if this ain't good fun!"

"Aye aye!" came a chorus of growly voices. "Good fun it is!"

"Does we get a little taste?" asked Toothy. "Just a little taste when they be cooked?"

Sniffy waved his wooden spoon in the air.

"Ooh - Miss Polly - Can us make some of them little crunchy crackers? I LOVES them!"

"NO!" Toothy flipped a spoonful of batter at Sniffy's head. "We wants choccy bikkies! LOTS of choccy bikkies!"

There was a loud growl from Long Jon Mustard.

"Custard creams is wot we wants! Choccy bikkies is RUBBISH!"

"CLUCK!" said Polly loudly, and flapped her wings, but no one took any notice.

Sniffy emptied his bowl over Long Jon Mustard's head, and Toothy Thomas rushed at them both waving his wooden spoon like a cutlass.

All the pirates let out whoops of joy and piled into the fight, tipping eggs and flour and sugar all over the deck.

"Watch out!" called Mutt as the struggling heap of pirates rolled dangerously close to where he was working.

"Careful, me hearties!" yelled Long Jon Mustard, and the writhing pile of bodies bundled itself down to the other end of the Ghastly Ghoul.

Polly Chicken and Jolly Roger looked at each other, and Roger shrugged. Captain Jenny frowned, and turned to Sea Dog Williams.

"Quick, Williams. See if you can stop them!"

"WOOF! WOOF! WOOF!" Sea Dog Williams leapt into the fray, skidded on the batter mixture and crashed into the mast.

"Wooo! Ow! Oooooh!" He sat and counted stars.

All around him pirates happily blipped and bopped each other. No one noticed Foxy Ratt slide over the side of the Ghastly Ghoul. He was wearing his water wings and carrying two cannon balls to weigh him down. He slipped into the water without a splash.

CHAPTER FOUR

Down and down and down Foxy went,
his sharp little eye peering all around
him. As he went deeper and deeper he
could see something glinting and
shining below him, and his evil heart
beat faster and faster. Landing on the
soft sand at the sea bottom he let go of
the cannon balls, grabbing and
snatching with both hands before he
was whizzed back to the surface by his
water wings. Arriving on the surface
with a POP! he stared greedily at his
booty.

There was no doubt about it. It was real, yellow, glistening glittering gold. Foxy opened his mouth to let out a whoop of joy and then closed it again quickly. What if he was seen? How could he hide his beautiful, wonderful gold? How could he keep it all for his very own self where no other horrible thieving pirate would find it?

Foxy rubbed his head and twisted round angrily. Who - or what - had hit him?

Behind him Sniffy's empty biscuit barrel bobbed merrily up and down on the waves.

"Ooo er!" Foxy said. "Just exactly wot I'm looking for or I'll be a coconut!" And he dropped his gold pieces inside the barrel. They fell in with a lovely CLINK! that made Foxy's beady little eye shine.

"Now," Foxy said to himself, "all I have to do is a few more dives and I'll be RICH! RICH! RICH! RICH! RICH!" And he began paddling himself silently back to the Ghastly Ghoul to collect more cannon balls.

There was little danger of Foxy being seen. On board the Ghastly Ghoul the battle was raging, with rolling pins and wooden spoons flying. Polly was perched up in the crow's nest squawking loudly, and Jenny and Roger were up there with her.

"Do you think," Jenny said with a sigh, "they've nearly finished fighting?"

Jolly Roger peered down. First Mate Mutt was still working away at his invention. All around him the deck was white with flour and covered with sprawling, sliding and writhing bodies.

"Doesn't look like it," said Roger. "Hey! Mutt's waving! I think he's finished his machine!"

"Then we'd better go back and take command!" said Captain Jennifer Jellyfish Jones, and she and Roger climbed rapidly down to the deck.

Polly, about to follow them, stopped. What was that she could see in the water? She shook her feathers, and flew out to look.

Foxy was on his way up from his umpteenth dive. He was very tired, but he was as happy as he had ever been. The barrel was splendidly full of gold and diamonds and rubies, and was floating noticeably deeper in the water.

"There ain't nothing much left down there," he muttered to himself. "When I gets back this time I'll sneak away in the old dinghy. Then it's OFF! And those namby pamby girlie captains can do without clever old Foxy Ratt!" And he cackled to himself.

Polly flew round in a circle. Peering down she could see Foxy's greasy head, and she could also see something glittering in the barrel.

"CLUCK!" said Polly, and flew back to report her findings.

CHAPTER FIVE

Captain Jennifer Jellyfish Jones and Jolly Roger stood side by side. Sea Dog Williams, rubbing his head with his paw, stood beside them. No one else was able to stand; the pirates, groaning and moaning and plastered with egg and flour and currants and butter and batter, lay exhausted on the deck.

Jenny took a deep breath and blew her whistle. Foxy Ratt, creeping up the anchor chain, froze.

"Well, well, well," Jenny said. "What shall we do with these miserable swabs? Shall we clap them in irons? Throw them to the sharks?"

"What about a little deck scrubbing to begin with?" Jolly Roger suggested.

"EXCELLENT idea," said Captain Jenny. "Maybe you and Sea Dog Williams could see to it."

"AYE AYE, CAP'N!" Jolly Roger and Sea Dog Williams snapped into action.

"Get mopping!"

"Woof! Woof! Woof!"

"And no flour and eggs in the sea! It'll attract sharks!"

"Woof! Woof! Woof! Woof!"

"JUMP TO IT!"

"WOOF! WOOF!"

"CLUCK! CLUCK CLUCKITTY CLUCK! CLUCK!"

"Grrr"!

Polly Chicken came flapping down and round and round Foxy Ratt as he hung on the anchor chain.

Roger glanced up. "What is it, Polly? Oh, it's you, is it, Foxy! Got knocked overboard, did you? Well - grab a mop and GET MOPPING!"

Foxy Ratt opened and shut his mouth several times, and then climbed back on board. His brain working overtime, he snatched up a mop and pretended to be busy.

"Got to get away!" he thought. "I've got to get away!" And as he thought he swilled gallons and gallons of the dirty grey biscuit mixture over the stern of the Ghastly Ghoul.

"HEY! STOP THAT, FOXY!" yelled Jolly Roger, but it was too late. It slid into the sea with a soft slurp, and apart from a few crumbs floating on the surface sank gently down and down. Foxy rubbed his hands together and threw away the mop. He didn't see the swirl in the water below as a hundred small fish came hurrying to gobble up their free dinner . . . and he didn't see the shoal of bigger fish that followed them a few minutes later.

Nor did he see the large
dark grey shape that
came swimming
slowly up to see
what was going
on, and stayed to
watch and see
what all the fuss
was about ...

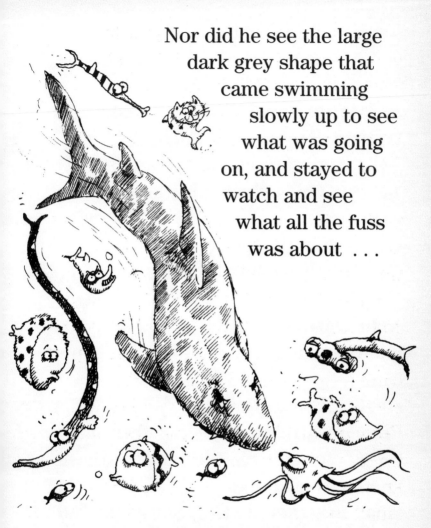

"Foxy," Roger said angrily, "come
here! It's bread and water for you for a
week!"

CHAPTER SIX

First Mate Mutt put down his
screwdriver with a last exhausted sigh.

"RIGHT!" he stood up and
stretched. "I think Mutt's supersonic
submergible submersible is ready for a
little action!"

"EH?" said Toothy.

"He means he's finished inventing
something to help us
get the treasure,"
Long Jon Mustard
said.

"Oh," said Toothy.
"I means, HURRAH!"

The pirates all
stopped scrubbing
and joined Jenny. They stared at Mutt's
submersible. It was made of two
biscuit barrels joined together, with
two hammocks slung below filled with

cannon balls. Portholes were cut into the barrels and milk bottles acted as glazing; two rubber glove hands stuck out from the first barrel and a knotted mass of ropes covered the whole invention. Out of the second barrel a long pipe trailed, while several buckets were attached to the sides.

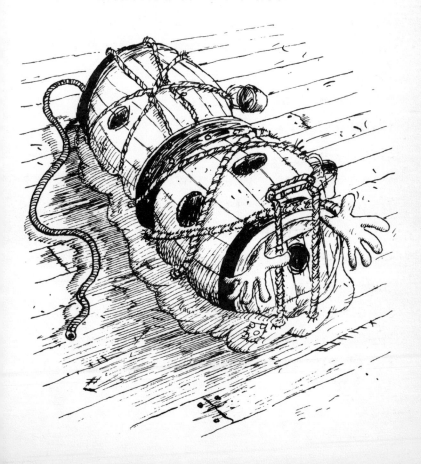

"AH!" said Jenny. "Well done, First Mate Mutt! Er . . . how does it work, exactly?"

First Mate Mutt took a deep breath.

"Submersible crew take up position in two barrels one to pick up treasure second to pump internal air pump to keep air fresh cannon balls to weight down submersible and keep it on sea bed close to treasure hoard buckets for filling with gold coins and diamonds and rubies and pearls and sending up to surface. Simple, really."

Jolly Roger shook his head. "Wouldn't it be easier if we just caught a few dolphins and trained them to bring up the gold for us? If we started now we'd probably have them ready in about ten years . . ."

First Mate Mutt looked offended. "It'll work perfectly," he said. "Just wait and see!"

Roger sighed. Captain Jenny shook Mutt's hand. "Excellent, Mutt. Who's going down in it?"

Mutt looked surprised. "Why, me of course. And I thought Foxy Ratt might like the job of pedalling the air pumps . . . seeing as Jolly Roger wasn't too peased with him just now."

Foxy stared, his face a sudden green. "ME?"

"That's right," said Mutt. He opened a small hatch in the second barrel. "In you hop!"

Foxy Ratt fell on his knees. "Cap'n! I begs you! Don't make me go in that there terrible contraption!" And he grovelled on the deck and tried to pat Jenny's boots.

"Woof!" said Sea Dog Williams, and he picked Foxy Ratt up by the scruff of the neck and dropped him neatly into the barrel.

"Well done, Sea Dog Williams!" said Mutt, and he snapped the hatch shut. Loud wails came from inside.

"It's all right," said Mutt comfortingly. "Once you're pedalling you won't have time to worry about anything else. Now for me." And he opened the hatch in the front barrel and stepped in. Almost.

"Oh," said Mutt.

"What is it?" asked Jenny.

"CLUCK!" said Polly.

"Well," said Mutt, "I think I underestimated the size of the crew member designed for this section."

"WOT?" asked Sniffy.

Long Jon Mustard let out a hoot of laughter. "He means as he's too fat!"

All the pirates began to laugh, and Mutt grinned as well.

"Dearie me," he said. "And me an inventor!"

Jolly Roger stepped forward. "If I volunteer," he said, "will everyone promise that I never, ever, EVER have to sing with the crew?"

Captain Jennifer Jellyfish Jones stood to attention and saluted Roger. "Pirate Captain's honour," she said. "And do be careful, Roger."

First Mate Mutt helped Roger fold himself into the barrel, and explained about putting his hands into the rubber gloves. Then he closed down the hatch.

"Crew ready!" he announced.

"Prepare to launch!"

Slowly and carefully the submersible was lowered down on its ropes. The weight of the cannon balls dragged it deeper and deeper until it was hovering just a few inches above the sea bed.

Roger, peering through his milk bottle portholes, tugged on the message rope. Up on board the Ghastly Ghoul Jenny looked anxious. "Are they all right?"

"They're fine!" said Mutt excitedly. "Now, hold everything exactly there! And wait for the first bucket of treasure!"

Inside the submersible Roger tried to make himself more comfortable and to see what was on the sea bed. The barrel had not been designed to fit someone as long as he was, and the view through the bottom of the milk bottles was restricted. Roger wondered gloomily if they would ever find anything at all. It seemed as if the sand was swirling all around them, and there were an extraordinary number of fish. He scrabbled at the sand with one of his gloved hands, and suddenly kicked his legs in thrilled excitement.

"OWWWWW!" came a wail from behind him.

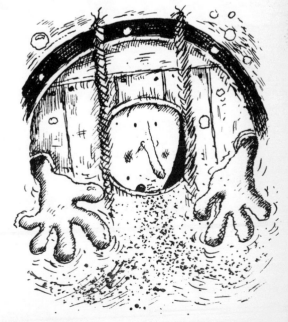

Roger twisted to shout over his shoulder.

"Sorry Foxy! I've

found something! And I'm certain this is where the treasure was . . . even though I can't quite see it . . . it feels HUGE! It might be a giant ruby . . . I'm putting it in the bucket. Oh - I've found another! And another . . ."

The submersible was rocking to and fro. Roger, desperately squinting through a bottle window, found himself looking at an eye. A large, loving eye. An eye that belonged to some enormous body that was trying hard to rub against the submersible in what could only be thought of as a very friendly manner.

Roger's mouth opened, but all that came out was a small squeak.

"WOT IS IT?" Foxy bawled from the back of the submersible, "WOT IS IT?"

Roger swallowed hard, and tried again. "It's a shark," he said.

"EEEEEEEKKK!" shrieked Foxy.

Up above on the Ghastly Ghoul First Mate Mutt was hauling up the first bucket. The crew were treading on each other's toes in a desperate effort to be the first to see the shine of real gold. Polly, flying in circles overhead, saw the bucket splash out of the water. At the same time she saw a sharp triangular black fin break the surface of the waves and then dive down again.

"CLUCK!" she squawked, "CLUCK!"

"I know, Polly," said Captain Jenny. "We're all excited . . . OH!"

They gazed disbelievingly at the contents of the bucket.

"STONES???? And two half bricks?? CANNON BALLS?"

CLUCKCLUCK CLUCKCLUCKKKK!!

Polly yelled at them, and pointed wildly with her wing at the ropes leading downwards to the submersible.

Jenny stared. "Are they in trouble, Polly?"

Jenny began taking off her sea boots. "I'm going down to see what's going on."

Polly danced up and down on the rail under Jenny's nose.

"I think she thinks that's a BAD idea!" said Mutt. "I think we should haul them up."

Polly was so pleased that someone, at last, was showing a little sense that she fainted clean away.

"Good gracious!" said Mutt, "Whatever's going on? Haul away, boys – and make it snappy."

The pirates hauled. And hauled. And hauled again.

"It seems MUCH heavier," Mutt said doubtfully.

Long Jon Mustard looked hopeful. "Maybe it's all that there treasure."

"H'mph," said Captain Jennifer.

"THREE... TWO... ONE... HEAVE!!!!!!"

"EEEEEEEEEKK!!!"

"Let's just give it one final heave. Put your backs into it, you feeble fishcakes - and maybe there'll be a reward at the end if it!"

"CLUCK!" said Polly feebly, and fainted again.

As the submersible came swinging up from the blue green water there was a universal shriek from all the pirates. Sitting on top was the most enormous shark that any of them had ever seen. It was murmuring sweet nothings into one of the portholes and patting the submersible hopefully with a fin. Jolly Roger's agonised eye could be seen wildly rolling at another porthole, and Foxy Ratt's yells echoed hollowly.

"Aha," Mutt said, and scratched his head. "We seem to have a problem."

"That ain't a problem," howled a white and trembling Toothy. "That be a SHARK!"

Sea Dog Williams began to bark loudly. They all turned to look at him, and saw that he was standing by a barrel.

"What is he on about?" asked Mutt.

Captain Jennifer Jellyfish Jones stared for a moment, and then waved her cutlass in the air.

"Quick, Mutt! The shark seems to think the submersible is the most beautiful thing it's ever seen . . . it's fallen in love with a barrel! If we throw all the other barrels into the sea it might follow them - at least, I hope so!!!!!"

As the first barrel hit the waves with a SPLASH the shark looked up. On board the Ghastly Ghoul, Jenny and Mutt held their breath. Polly opened one eye.

The shark opened its huge jaws wide and smiled. Its dagger sharp teeth shone, and the pirates clutched each other in terror.

"SPLASH!" Sea Dog Williams pushed another barrel overboard.

It bobbed up and down behind the first one, and the shark looked puzzled. It shook its head, and patted the submersible.

"SPLASH!" A third barrel rolled off the Ghastly Ghoul. It was too much for the shark. It winked roguishly at the barrels as they floated past and dived off. With a loud cheer Mutt gave the signal to haul the submersible on board.

SPLASH!!

CHAPTER SEVEN

Jolly Roger crawled out, and Foxy Ratt
staggered behind him. They collapsed
on the deck, and groaned.

"What did we find?" Roger asked
faintly. "I put a few things in the
bucket. They were pretty big. Were
they rubies?"

Captain Jenny
shook her head.
"Sorry, Roger.
Only cannon balls.
Just the same as
ours, actually."
She held one out
for Roger to see,
and then grabbed
it back and peered
closely at it.
"EXACTLY the
same as ours!

AND it's got GG
on it . . ."

Foxy Ratt
suddenly stopped
groaning and
began to whistle in
an "I'm all right
now and I don't
know ANYTHING
about what's being
said" sort of way.

Jenny gave him a thoughtful glance.

"It was all there was," Roger said. "I
MUST have been seeing things before,
although I really thought it was real. It
was very odd - I couldn't see anything
glittering at all . . . it was so cloudy and
there were MILLIONS of fish swimming
about."

Foxy Ratt got up, and sauntered to
the rail of the Ghastly Ghoul. Trying to
look as if he was breathing in the fine

fresh air he squinted over the side. Was his precious barrel still safely out there? He was certain he could trick his wily way away . . . away to GOLD and RICHES and TREASURE!!

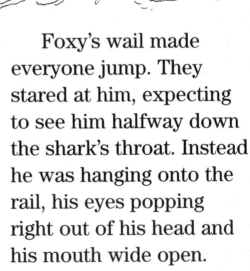

Foxy's wail made everyone jump. They stared at him, expecting to see him halfway down the shark's throat. Instead he was hanging onto the rail, his eyes popping right out of his head and his mouth wide open.

"Is it a ghostie?" asked Toothy, his voice shaky.

"He's seen a wampire for sure," said Long Jon Mustard.

"Ooooooooooooooh!" trembled Sniffy. "What is it, Foxy?"

"I think," said Captain Jennifer Jellyfish Jones, "Foxy Ratt has seen the shark. He's seen the shark making friends with a barrel . . . a barrel that looks as if it's floating rather low in the water. And he's watching the shark play nudge nudge wink wink with the barrel . . . and for SOME REASON this is making Foxy feel VERY STRANGE. Perhaps Foxy would like to tell us ALL why he's feeling this way?"

Foxy Ratt shut his mouth like a steel trap. "Ain't nothing, Cap'n," he said in a strangled voice. "I ain't interested in no barrels. I was just a . . . a watching of that 'orrible shark."

"Good," said Jenny. "Long Jon Mustard, Toothy and Sniffy – I've got a little job for you. Pick up a couple of those cannon balls. Let's see if you can toss them into that barrel . . . the barrel Foxy isn't at all interested in. Maybe we could sink it!"

Foxy turned green, and then white, and then pale purple. He fell on his knees. "No!" he whispered. "No!"

"I think," said Captain Jennifer Jellyfish Jones, "we'd better see what exactly IS in that barrel . . . but we must be careful of the shark. We'll sail the Ghastly Ghoul alongside, and have just a little peep! ALL HANDS ON DECK! PULL UP THE ANCHOR!!!!!"

An hour later the entire crew of the Ghastly Ghoul were very, VERY happy. Toothy had diamonds in his hair, and Sniffy was trying to balance a ruby in his tummy button. Jenny and Roger and Mutt were dividing out gold coins, and Polly was helping Long Jon Mustard count to five. Sea Dog Williams was busy elsewhere on deck.

He was keeping guard on a thin and unhappy prisoner. A thin and unhappy prisoner wearing an apron. A thin and unhappy prisoner unwillingly mixing and stirring and making crunchy crackers. And custard creams. And lots and lots and LOTS of choccy bikkies …